CLICK GO THE SHEARS

CLICK

© Illustrations Robert Ingpen 1984
First published 1984 by William Collins Pty Ltd, Sydney
First published in paperback 1986
Typeset by Savage & Co Pty Ltd, Brisbane
Printed By Dai Nippon Printing Co (Hong Kong) Ltd

National Library of Australia
Cataloguing-in-Publication data

Click go the shears

For children.
ISBN 0 00 662326 3

1. Ballads, Australian — Juvenile literature
I. Ingpen, Robert, 1936-

A 821'.044

GO THE SHEARS

ILLUSTRATED BY ROBERT INGPEN

FONTANA PICTURE LIONS
Collins Australia

The Shearer's Life

In his classic book *On the Wool Track*, with its graphic pictures of station life in Australia nearly a century ago, C. E. W. Bean describes the shearers as a 'republic'. They are wandering men, who in those days travelled the rough bush tracks from shearing shed to shearing shed on foot, on horseback, or even by bicycle — sometimes with tyres filled with grass or patched with kangaroo hide because they were punctured so often. Usually they wrote to the stations well in advance, to book their 'stands'. Once assembled, they elected a representative or 'boss' who would stand between them and the station owner, and who would decide on every issue: from whether the cook was fit to cook to whether the sheep were in a fit condition to shear. It was a rough and ready democracy, stemming from the deep-rooted traditions of Australian mateship and independence and reflected in some aspects of modern politics.

The shearer has his place in Australian folklore, and in retrospect wears a romantic aura, but his life was a hard one. Shearing was usually done in hot conditions, with the men working in a stooping position, breathing air thick with dust and handling wet or dirty sheep. There was a competitive atmosphere in which men felt that they must strive to outdo each other in order to become the 'ringer' of the shed. Yet there is no industry in which the product could be more seriously affected by unskilled work.

The shearers came in all shapes and sizes. 'Old men, young men, tall men, short men, fine straight upstanding men, delicate men, strong faces, weak faces, clean faces, sodden faces, men in every sort of coat and jersey, in old boots, in new boots, men with patched pants, men with their pants tucked into their socks, men with their trousers stained and frayed, men with their trousers creased and turned up,' as Bean described them. But they all had three things in common. One was the softness of their hands, on which the skin was as soft as a fine lady's because of its constant cleaning and softening by the lanoline in the wool fleeces. Another was the skill with which they peeled the fleeces off the sheep with hand shears and later mechanical clippers. And thirdly, the habit they had for drinking their earnings in the bars of country pubs along the roads between stations and in dusty outback towns.

Out on the board the old shearer stands,
Grasping his shears in his long, bony hands,
Fixed is his gaze on a bare-bellied 'joe',
Glory if he gets her, won't he make the ringer go.

Chorus

Click go the shears boys, click, click, click,
Wide is his blow and his hands move quick,
The ringer looks around and is beaten by a blow,
And curses the old snagger with the blue-bellied 'joe'.

In the middle of the floor in his cane-bottomed chair
Is the boss of the board, with his eyes everywhere;
Notes well each fleece as it comes to the screen,
Paying strict attention if it's taken off clean.

The colonial-experience man, he is there, of course,
With his shiny leggin's, just got off his horse,
Casting round his eye like a real connoisseur,
Whistling the old tune, 'I'm the Perfect Lure'.

The tar-boy is there, awaiting in demand,
With his blackened tar-pot, and his tarry hand;
Sees one old sheep with a cut upon its back,
Hears what he's waiting for, 'Tar here, Jack!'

Shearing is all over and we've all got our cheques,
Roll up your swag for we're off on the tracks;
The first pub we come to, it's there we'll have a spree,
And everyone that comes along it's,
        'Come and drink with me!'

Down by the bar the old shearer stands,
Grasping his glass in his thin bony hands;
Fixed is his gaze on a green-painted keg,
Glory, he'll get down on it, ere he stirs a peg.

There we leave him standing, shouting for all hands,
Whilst all around him every 'shouter' stands;
His eyes are on the cask, which is now lowering fast,
He works hard, he drinks hard,
    and goes to hell at last!

Arr. by Sophie Ingpen

Out on the board the- old shea-rer stands,

Gras-ping his shears in his thin bon-y hands,

Fixed is his gaze on a bare-bell-ied 'joe',

Glory if he gets her, won't he make the ringer go.

Chorus

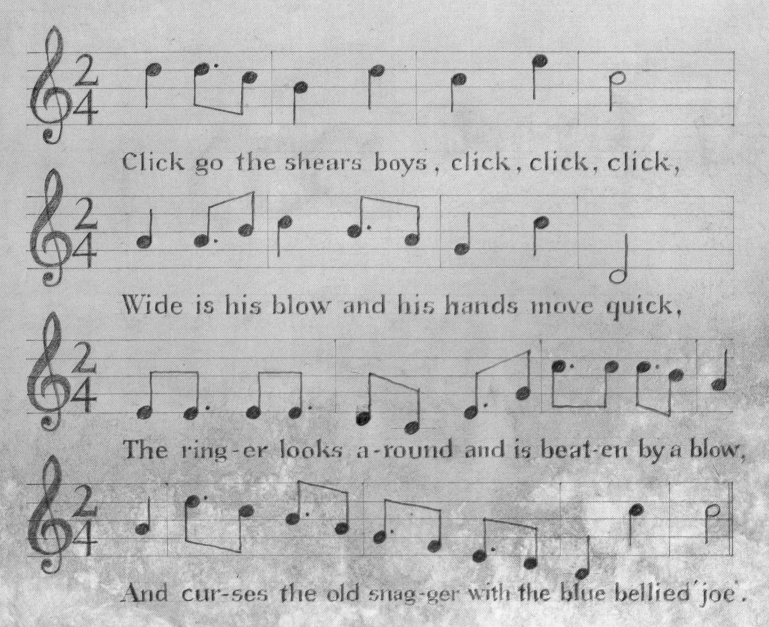

Click go the shears boys, click, click, click,

Wide is his blow and his hands move quick,

The ring-er looks a-round and is beat-en by a blow,

And cur-ses the old snag-ger with the blue bellied 'joe'.